Weed Management in Direct-Seeded Rice Under Cambodian Conditions

T0396668

Weed Management in Direct-Seeded Rice Under Cambodian Conditions

Robert J. Martin
Pao Srean
Daniel K Y Tan

ELIVA PRESS

ISBN: 978-99949-8-799-3

Cover Design: Eliva Press
Cover Image: Ingimage
Email: info@elivapress.com
Website: www.elivapress.com

This Eliva Press imprint is published by the registered company Eliva Press
Global Ltd. part of Eliva Press S.R.L. Publishing Group

The registered company address is: Pope Hennessy Street Level 2, Hennessy
Tower Port Louis, Mauritius
Eliva Press S.R.L. Publishing Group address is: Bulevardul Moscova 21,
Chisinau, Moldova, Europe

Weed management in direct-seeded rice under Cambodian conditions

Dr Robert J Martin

Director, Agricultural Systems Research (Cambodia) Co Ltd, Battambang, Cambodia

Dr Pao Srean

Dean, Faculty of Agriculture and Food Processing, National University of Battambang, Cambodia

Professor Daniel K Y Tan

School of Life and Environmental Sciences, University of Sydney, Sydney, Australia

Figure 1. *Leptochloa chinensis*, a common weed of rice fields.

Contents

Summary

In Cambodia, the increasing scarcity of rural labour is pushing farmers to find ways to manage large rice fields with meagre resources and continuously emerging crop management constraints, especially for weed control. Out-migration of rural labour has resulted in a shift from manual transplanting to direct-seeded rice (DSR) and this has changed the spectrum of weed species and made weed management more difficult in rice. This publication describes important weeds of rice in Cambodia, weed seed contamination in rice seed for sowing, weedy rice contamination in paddy and options for Integrated Weed Management (IWM). The elements of IWM include: cultural practices; stale seedbed; crop establishment methods; crop rotation; water management and chemical weed control. Modernisation of weed management in Cambodia, is constrained by a lack of uptake of existing published research and failure to incorporate results of new research into extension media. Multiple conflicting messages emanating from Donors and Non-Governmental Organisations (NGOs) also confuse farmers and delay adoption of good agricultural practices (GAP). Furthermore, in the absence of a functioning public extension service, Cambodian farmers are locked into pesticide-reliant practices and limited use of alternatives. Pesticide manufacturers, distributors and local sellers reinforce pesticide-based recommendations as the dominant technology. In Cambodia, weed research priorities include development of: management practices to reduce weed seed banks in direct-seeded rice fields; integrated weed management strategies to delay or avoid development of herbicide resistance in major weed species in direct-seeded rice; options for the integrated management of weedy rice (*Oryza sativa* f. spontanea) in direct-seeded rice; and comparison of Unmanned Aerial Vehicles (UAVs) with ground application for efficacy and safety of herbicide application in rice.

Introduction

With the increasing scarcity of rural labour, Cambodian farmers are pushed to find ways to manage large rice fields with meagre resources and continuously emerging crop management constraints. Cambodia has 3.7 million hectares of agricultural land and 76% of this is planted with lowland rice, while only 24% is planted to other crops (Martin 2020). In the past, the labour for rice production was provided by members of family or neighbouring farm households. However, these options have decreased because of out-migration of rural labour with more than 50% of out-migration going to construction (32%) and garment factories (20%) (Chhim et al. 2015). With lack of available labour and increased production costs, farmers are shifting from manual transplanting to direct-seeded rice (DSR) or mechanical transplanting systems (Chauhan 2012, Figure 2).

Figure 2. Rice field planted with the Thai Kid seed drill in 2021.

Direct wet seeded rice (DSR) offers advantages of faster and easier planting, reduced labour requirement, shorter crop duration, increased water-use efficiency and greater profit (Kachroo and Bazaya, 2011). In the shift to this system however, farmers face emerging problems such as achieving effective weed control (Figure 3).

Figure 3. *Echinochloa* spp. are important weeds of DSR in Cambodia

Direct seeding systems for rice are either dry seeded, wet seeded or water seeded (Chauhan 2012). A common technique for seeding is broadcasting of seed by hand. This is perceived to be easy to implement and expectedly results in shorter turn-around time for rice intensification in areas with supplementary irrigation (Beecher et al. 2014). Broadcast dry seeding (non-pre-germinated seeds) on dry seedbeds (non-saturated) and wet seeding (pre-germinated seeds) on saturated or puddled soils is common in Cambodia (Ikeda et al. 2008). Hand broadcasting has long been practiced by farmers in some provinces such as Battambang province (Nesbitt and Chan 1997). However, farmers in other provinces such as Takeo have recently switched from transplanting to hand broadcasting (Martin 2020). Weeds are a significant biotic constraint to the sustainability and profitability of DSR systems (Chauhan et al. 2015). There are also impacts from the recent expansion of DSR, and the associated weed management practices. Excessive and inefficient use of herbicides and the limited access to irrigation have been found to cause a shift in weed species composition from aquatic species to grasses and sedges in DSR ecosystems (Martin et al. 2020).

Weeds cause greater yield losses in DSR systems compared to transplanted rice systems because of the size differential between rice and weed seedlings, the absence of suppressive effect of standing water on weed emergence, absence of competitive advantage in transplanted rice seedlings and weed growth at crop emergence (Chauhan 2012). The inability to control water levels in rice fields during the planting season in Cambodia also contributes to the difficulty with weed management (Matsukawa et al. 2016). The extent of yield loss is affected by cultural methods, rice variety, weed species present, and the density and duration of weed competition (Singh et al. 2014).

Hand weeding has been the conventional way to suppress weed populations in rice field (Khaliq et al. 2012, Chauhan et al. 2015). However, hand weeding is labour intensive, difficult to implement on time when there is shortage of labour and also incurs high costs (Singh et al. 2016).

Figure 4. Weeds should be removed before they set seed.

Herbicides are considered to be an economic alternative for weed control compared with hand weeding (Singh et al. 2014). Herbicides used to control weeds in rice can be applied as pre-emergence or post-emergence options (Chauhan et al. 2015). When pre-emergence herbicides fail to control weeds, post-emergence herbicide or hand weeding are still needed (Singh et al. 2014). Post-emergence herbicide application is often required to control weed escapes from pre-emergence herbicide application in DSR (Khaliq et al. 2012).

Farmers often prefer single application of pre- or post-emergence herbicides but this approach does not always effectively control diverse weed flora (Singh et al. 2016). Most herbicide applications target specific weed species and are often effective on a narrow range of weed species. Repeated application of herbicides within the same mode of action (MoA) group might also result in weed flora shift and development of herbicide resistance (Rawat et al. 2012). Jabran and Chauhan (2015) documented several weed species that have evolved resistance to a number of herbicides. The intensive use of herbicides has resulted in the appearance of herbicide resistant weeds species. Two hundred and twenty weed species have evolved resistance to one or more herbicides, and there are now 404 unique cases (species × site of action) of herbicide-resistant weeds globally (Heap 2014).

Herbicides are important tools in DSR systems but excessive use and misuse of herbicides can result in unintended negative consequences for effective weed management. There is a need to test options for suitable and locally-adapted recommendations for weed management problems faced by Cambodian farmers. The efficacy of potential recommended weed management options need to be validated to encourage farmers to adopt more effective herbicide practices.

This publication describes important weeds of rice in Cambodia, weed seed contamination in rice seed for sowing, weedy rice contamination in paddy and options for integrated weed management (IWM). The elements of IWM include: cultural practices; stale seedbed; crop establishment methods; crop rotation; water management and chemical weed control.

Important weeds of direct-seeded rice in Cambodia

Ninety-three per cent of rice farmers in Battambang province say that weed management is a major problem in their fields, and only 16% report a low level of infestation. The majority of farmers (55%) claim that yield loss from weeds is >25%, and only 7% of farmers report low yield loss (5–10%) due to weeds (Chhun et al. 2020). At 250 USD/t and an average paddy yield of 3 t/ha, yield losses of 10%–25% cost 75–190 USD/ha. In Battambang province, 98% of farmers report weeds as a major problem in wet-seeded rice whereas only 88% of farmers report weeds as a major problem in dry-seeded rice. According to Battambang farmers, the 10 most important weed species affecting rice are *Echinochloa crus-galli, Echinochloa colona, Melochia corchorifolia, Cyperus iria, Leptochloa chinensis, Fimbristylis miliacea, Oryza sativa* f. *spontanea, Cyperus difformis, Cyanotis axillaris* and *Ischaeum rugosum* (Martin et al. 2021, Figure 5).

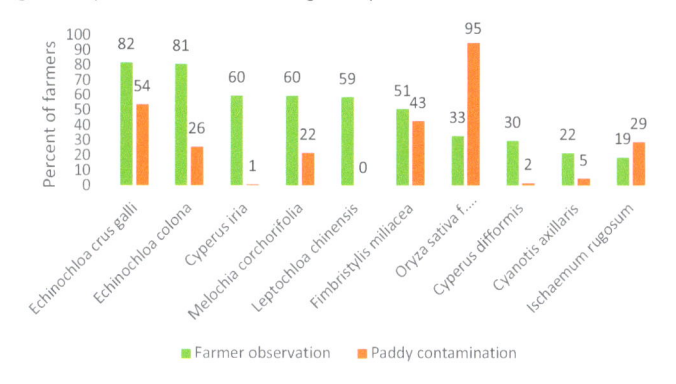

Figure 5. The 10 most important weeds of rice in North-West Cambodia according to farmers (%) and the presence of their seeds in harvested paddy (%).

Description, importance and management for common weeds of direct-seeded rice

Commelinaceae: *Cyanotis axillaris* **(L.) D. Don ex Sweet (Slab Tea)**

Description

Perennial herb. Stems succulent, creeping and rooting at the lower nodes. Leaves linear-lanceolate. Flowers solitary and axillary, with 3 petals, purple to violet. Capsule oblong, trigonous, 4–5 mm. Seeds grey-brown, pitted, 1.5–2 mm long.

Importance

Common weed seed contaminant in harvested rice paddy.

Management

Cultural control*:* Uproot plants and destroy them; ensure clean seed for sowing.

Cyperaceae: *Cyperus difformis* **L. (Kok Chruk Touch)**

Description

Annual herb to around 30 cm in height. Inflorescence a rounded bundle 1-3 cm wide, with up to 120 spikelets. Achenes are 0.6–0.8 mm long and 0.3–0.4 mm wide, triangular, yellowish-brown.

Importance

Produces large quantities of seed and can complete its life cycle in 30 days. Dominant weed in DSR. Can cause rice yield losses of 12–50%.

Management

Cultural control: Hand and mechanical weeding in row-planted rice crops can provide effective control.

Chemical control: Bentazon, butachlor, 2,4-D, MCPA, pretilachlor, propanil, and thiobencarb reported to be effective.

Cyperaceae: *Cyperus iria* L. (Kok Chruk)

Description

Annuals. Roots fibrous. Culms tufted, 8–80 cm tall. Achene dark brown, obovoid, 1.2–1.4 mm.

Importance

Weed of open, wet places, wetland rice. Important weed of dry direct-seeded rice fields.

Management

Cultural control: Hand weeding at earlier stage of growth to prevent flowering and seed production.

Chemical control: Butachlor for dry-seeded and pretilachlor for wet-seeded rice applied 0-3 days after sowing (DAS).

Cyperaceae: *Fimbristylis miliacea* (L.) Vahl (Kok Phneak Kdam)

Description

Tufted glabrous annual, 10–40 cm. Stem 0.8–1.2 mm diameter, usually triangular. Achene 0.5–0.6 x 0.3–0.4 mm, globular.

Importance

Common weed of dry direct-seeded rice. Alternative host for some diseases of rice, Important wood seed contaminant of harvested rice paddy.

Management

Cultural control: Planting weed-free seed.

Chemical control: Post-emergence application of 2,4-D.

Malvaceae: *Melochia corchorifolia* L. (Krachib)

Description

Herbs or subshrubs, less than 1 m tall, erect or decumbent. Capsule globose, 5-angular, 5–6 mm in diameter. Seeds 1 or 2 per cell, brown-black, ovoid, slightly triangular, 2–3 mm.

Importance

It is a common and important weed of rice. It is an important weed seed contaminant in rice paddy kept for replanting.

Management

Cultural control: Planting weed-free seed.

Chemical control: Pre-emergence, pretilachlor; post-emergence, 2,4-D, bensulfuron methyl.

Poaceae: *Echinochloa colona* (L.) Link (Kmean Kantuy)

Description

Annual grass. Tufted, erect and jointed, often flat on the ground, and 30–60 cm high. Reddish-purple or green. Seed head is a panicle with 3–10 branches 5–15 cm long. Spikelets plumply ovate-oblong, 2–3 mm,

Importance

It closely "mimics" rice in the vegetative growth stage and is a severe competitor of rice. It is a host of diseases such as tungro and rice yellow dwarf.

Management

Cultural control: Hand weeding or use of a hoe during early growth stages.

Chemical control: Pre-emergence application of butachlor or pretilachlor, or post-emergence application of cyhalofop, butachlor, and fenoxaprop can be effective.

Poaceae: *Echinochloa crus-galli* (L.) Beauv. (Smao Bek Kbal)

Description

Annual. Culms coarse, erect or geniculately ascending, 20–150 cm tall. Spikelets green or purplish, ovate. Fertile floret 2.5–3.0 mm, ellipsoid, glabrous, glossy, cream-brown.

Importance

Serious weed of lowland rice due to its rapid growth, competitive ability, and capacity to multiply rapidly. A serious weed seed contaminant in harvested rice paddy.

Management

Cultural control: Thorough land preparation for rice under wet or dry conditions can reduce infestations.

Chemical control: Pre-emergence butachlor, pretilachlor, or post-emergence cyhalofop, quinclorac, fenoxaprop.

Poaceae: *Ischaemum rugosum* Salisb. (Smao Srauv)

Description

Erect or ascending annual or perennial; up to 100 cm. Stem purplish, hairs at nodes. Paired terminal spikes pressed against one another. At maturity, it separates into two spike-like racemes. Sessile spikelet yellowish green, up to 6 mm long, first glume prominently transversely wrinkled; awns spiral at base, dark coloured.

Importance

Serious weed in lowland direct-seeded rice, emerges later than other weeds and is favoured by shallow flooding. Serious weed seed contaminant of harvested rice paddy.

Management

Cultural control: Planting seed free of weed seeds.

Chemical control: Pre-emergence butachlor, pretilachlor; or post-emergence cyhalofop, quinclorac, fenoxaprop.

Poaceae: *Leptochloa chinensis* **(L.) Nees. (Smao Kantouy Knou)**

Description

Annual or perennial to 120 cm tall. Inflorescence narrowly ovate, loose panicle, 10–40 cm long, with many spike-like slender branches. Spikelets 2–3.2 mm long, purplish or green and 4–6 flowered. Caryopsis 0.5–1.0 mm, ovoid, glabrous, orange-brown.

Importance

Serious weed of rice. Its ability to withstand waterlogged conditions as well as drained, moist conditions makes it a problem weed in rice.

Management

Cultural control: Rotovating and puddling of rice fields during land preparation; hand weeding can be effective during the early growth stages of the weed.

Chemical control: Pre-emergence butachlor, pretilachlor; or post-emergence cyhalofop, quinclorac, fenoxaprop. Avoid bispyribac-sodium.

Poaceae: *Oryza sativa* **f.** *spontanea* **Rosh. (Muk Chagae)**

Description

Usually taller than cultivated rice. Highly variable with awned or awnless spikelets. Spikelets vary in colour from cream to dark brown., It commonly possesses red pericarp.

Importance

Requires additional milling to remove red pericarp, thereby reducing the quality of milled rice. In Battambang province, 95% of harvested paddy contains seeds of weedy rice.

Management

Cultural control: Planting clean seed, hand rogueing before panicles mature.

Chemical control: Pre-emergence application of pretilachlor + fenclorim or butachlor + fenclorim.

Farmer rankings for the importance of weed species vary between rainfed and irrigated conditions and for dry seeding vs wet seeding (Figure 6, Figure 7). Under rainfed and dry seeding conditions, *F. miliacea, O. sativa* f *spontanea* and *C. iria* are the main problem, whereas under irrigated and wet seeding conditions, *E. crus-galli* and *L. chinensis* are ranked as the most serious weed problems. According to farmers, weed species that are becoming an increasing problem include *C. iria*, *E. crus-galli*, *E. colona*, *Fimbristylis* spp., *L. chinensis* and *O. sativa* f. *spontanea*. *F. miliacea*, *O. sativa* and *E. crus-galli* contaminate rice seed for sowing whereas *C. iria* and *L. chinensis* do not (Martin et al. 2017).

Figure 6. Comparison of weed species rankings under rainfed and irrigated conditions.

Figure 7. Comparison of weed species rankings under dry and wet seeding conditions.

Weed seed contamination in rice seed for sowing

In a survey of 100 freshly harvested rice paddy samples in Battambang province, Chhun et al. (2020) found contamination from seeds of 34 different weed species, from 12 plant families. The nine most important weed seed contaminants in harvested paddy are shown in. Figure 8.

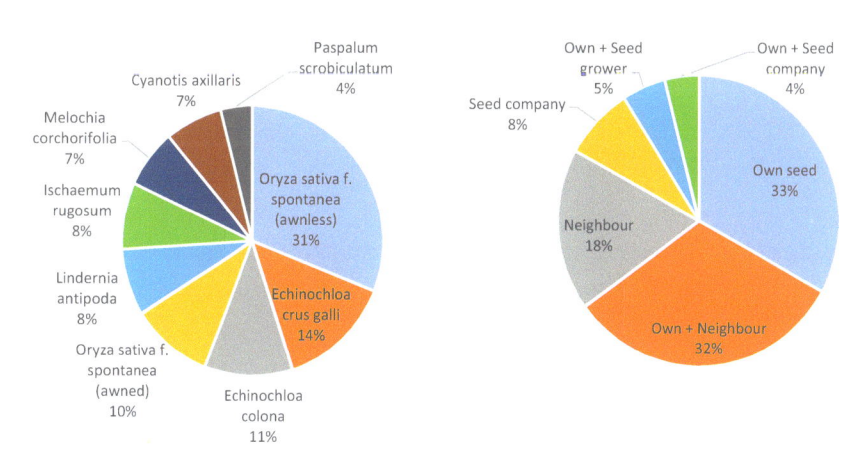

Figure 8. Major weed seed contaminants in rice seed (% of samples).

Figure 9. Source of seed for sowing in Battambang.

Eighty-three per cent of seed for sowing is farm-kept seed, but 17% of farmers use at least some commercial seed (Figure 9).

Rice seed kept for sowing by farmers is likely to be heavily contaminated with weed seeds. On average, a kilo of rice seed contains 355 weedy rice seeds and 241 weed seeds (Figure 10). Consequently, at a seeding rate of 180 kg/ha, an average of 6.4 weedy rice seeds and 4.4 seeds of other weed species are sown per square metre.

Martin et al. (2017) found that 85% of farmers winnow seed kept for sowing, 27% use the flotation method and 19% use both (Figure 10). Farmers are able to significantly reduce weed seeds in the paddy but are not successful in removing weedy rice seeds from paddy (Figure 12).

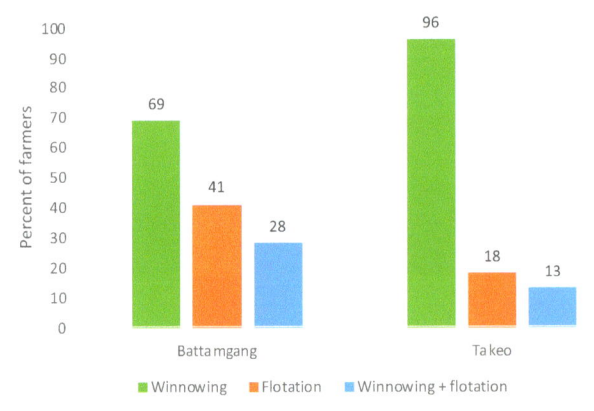

Figure 10. Seed-cleaning methods used by farmers in Battambang and Takeo provinces.

Weedy rice contamination in paddy

Weedy rice (*Oryza sativa* f. *spontanea*) is the product of interspecific hybridization between wild rice species such as *Oryza rufipogon* and cultivated rice (Wongtamee et al. 2017). Wild rice is a perennial grass that commonly occurs in drains and around ponds close to cultivated rice fields and was the predominant grass species in the seasonally flooded natural grasslands surrounding the Tonle Sap lake before the beginning of modern rice cultivation in Cambodia (Davidson 2006). In a 2017 survey, almost all farmers were familiar with weedy rice (99%) but only 35% of farmers said that weedy rice was a problem in their fields (Martin et al. 2017). However, in the seed contamination study it was found that 94% of paddy samples kept for sowing were contaminated with weedy rice with 91% of samples containing seeds of awnless and 57% containing seeds of awned weedy rice. This suggests that farmers, as well as professionals, might have difficulty distinguishing between varietal off-types and awnless weedy rice biotypes in rice fields.

Weedy rice phenotypes vary in height, time to maturity and degree of spikelet shattering. Spikelets can be awned or awnless and vary in colour from cream to almost black. The pericarp of awnless biotypes are red at maturity whereas pericarps of awned biotypes are usually yellow or pale green at maturity but turn red with age. Weedy rice biotypes vary according to the cultivated variety. Spikelets of weedy rice in variety Sen Kra-ob fields are shorter and fatter than Sen Kra-ob spikelets and can be removed by locally-designed seed cleaning machines. In other varieties such as Neang Khon, weedy rice spikelets can be the same size or larger than the crop spikelets. Examples of the variability of weedy rice spikelets are shown in Figure 11.

Figure 11. Examples of variability in spikelets and caryopses of weedy rice
(awnless biotypes above and awned biotypes below).

Experienced inspectors can detect weedy rice in paddy samples but inspection should include de-hulling in the laboratory to check for grains with red pericarps. Martin et al. (2017) found that farmers could significantly reduce weed seeds in rice seed for sowing by on-farm cleaning (Figure 12). However, on-farm cleaning did not significantly reduce the level of weedy rice contamination (Figure 12). Furthermore, average levels of weed seed and weedy rice contamination in seed producer seed did not meet certification standards (Table 1).

Table 1. Rice seed standards for respective seed classes in Cambodia (Khun and Soly 2012)

Contaminant	Breeder seed	Foundation seed	Registered seed	Certified seed
Weed seeds per 500 g (Max.)	3	5	10	10
Red rice per 500 g (Max.)	0	1	3	5

Figure 12. Levels of weedy rice contamination in fresh paddy, farm seed kept for sowing and in seed producer seed.

Integrated weed management

Farmers are encouraged to manage weeds using an integrated weed management (IWM) approach that combines all available options. The aims should be to keep the weed numbers low and prevent weeds from producing seeds throughout the cropping cycle.

Farmers have the option to manage weeds in advance before the crop is sown (Figure 13). This prevents weeds from setting seeds in the previous crop or fallow. Weeds should be controlled around the edge of the field, along waterways and in adjacent non-cropped areas. Planting with seed free of weed seeds is also part of IWM.

May	Jun	Jul	Aug	Sep	Oct	Nov	Dec	Jan	Feb	Mar	Apr
Dry-seeded rice					Wet-seeded rice				Stale seedbed or cover crop		

Activities (shown as vertical labels across the calendar):
- Clean planting machines
- Clean seed for sowing
- Plant with row or drill planter
- Apply pre-emergence herbicide
- Apply post-emergence herbicide
- Manage water level in field if possible
- Hand-weed as required
- Hand-roguing weeds at anthesis
- Clean harvesting machines
- Clean seed for sowing
- Plant with row or drill planter
- Apply pre-emergence herbicide
- Apply post-emergence herbicide
- Manage water level in field if possible
- Hand-weed as required
- Hand-roguing weeds at anthesis
- Clean harvesting machines
- Control weeds around the field
- Don't plough the field
- Retain weed seeds at the soil surface
- Prevent weeds from setting seed
- Apply pre-sowing herbicide
- Minimise tillage before planting

Figure 13. Example of a weed management calendar for rice.

Cultural practices

A decline in the availability of agricultural labour has resulted in rapid mechanisation of land preparation, broadcast seeding replacing transplanting, herbicide use and mechanised harvesting of rice. These changes have had significant repercussions for weed management. The main weed management challenges are associated with rice crop intensification, transition from transplanting to DSR, changed planting dates and tillage practices in response to climate change, over-reliance on post-emergence herbicides, excessive inversion tillage and lack of knowledge about the safe and efficacious application of herbicides.

Managing weeds in DSR systems is a challenging and worsening problem for farmers in North-West Cambodia. Cultural weed management approaches can help reduce the problem, including:

- using the stale-seedbed technique to reduce the weed seed bank and weed density in the crop
- using rice seeds free from weed and weedy rice seeds for planting
- cleaning farm implements before moving them from field to field.

Stale seedbed

There are different versions of the stale-seedbed technique depending on the type of rice system. In North-West Cambodia, rice is predominantly harvested by combine machine and, typically, 100–200 kg/ha of harvested rice seed is returned to the field. These seeds, plus harvested weed seeds, are added to the seed bank if the field is inversion-ploughed after harvest.

Mulching of the crop residues retains self-sown rice and weed seeds at the soil surface where they can readily germinate after intermittent rainfall events during the dry season

(Figure 14, Figure 15). These weeds are controlled using a non-selective herbicide such as glyphosate before they set seed. Further cultivation before planting rice should be avoided to preserve soil water and to prevent dormant weed seeds from being brought to the surface at planting time.

Figure 14. Heavy-duty mulching machines retain crop residues and weed seeds at the soil surface.

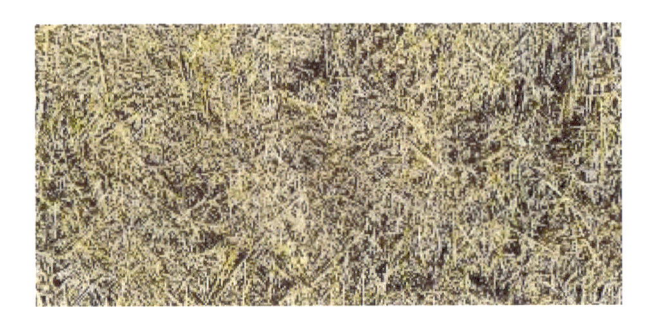

Figure 15. Stale seedbeds retain crop residues and weed seeds at the soil surface.

Crop establishment methods

Alternative crop establishment methods to manage weeds in DSR in North-West Cambodia include the following:

- *High seeding rates*. The use of high seeding rates may help to suppress weeds. However, it is expensive compared to alternative options and could encourage farmers to use cheap weed-infested seed which would defeat the purpose.
- *Row-seeding*. Row-seeded rice has an advantage over broadcast rice as weedy rice seedlings emerging between the rows can be easily distinguished. In row-seeded rice, manual and mechanical weeding is possible.
- *Flooding*. Appropriate timing, duration and depth of flooding can be used in managing weedy rice and other weeds in DSR systems. However, farmers in North-West Cambodia have little control over water management.

Crop rotation

Continuous cropping of rice with similar management practices allows weed seed banks to build in the soil. Alternative crops with different management practices and herbicide options can help disrupt the growth cycle of weeds. Therefore, a crop rotation is considered to be an effective control measure for problematic weed species. Where soil and water conditions permit, rice can be rotated with an upland crop such as maize, soybean, sesame or mungbean. However, Cambodian rice soils are often a hostile environment for rotational crops without supplementary irrigation. For example, strong hardpans prevent root growth below 15–20 cm on Toul Samroung soil.

Mungbean (*Vigna radiata* (L.) R. Wilczek) or Sunn hemp (*Crotalaria juncea* L.) can be direct-seeded as cover crops into rice crop residues at the end of the wet season (Figure 16, Figure 17). It is important that crop residues are retained at the soil surface to preserve soil moisture and lower soil surface temperature.

Figure 16. Mungbean planted into rice residues with minimal soil disturbance.

The amount of biomass produced by cover crops will vary depending on the amount of rain from occasional storms during the dry season. Apart from contributing to soil organic matter, legume cover crops increase soil fertility by biological nitrogen fixation.

Figure 17. Sunn hemp (*Crotalaria juncea* L.).

Chemical weed control

Chemical weed control is the use of herbicides to kill or inhibit weed growth. Chemical weed control is an option in IWM that should be combined with cultural, manual and mechanical control methods. Advantages of herbicides include reduced cost of labour, cost-effectiveness, more timely weed control and selective control of weeds especially at early growth stages of the crop.

Effective use of herbicides is limited by lack of understanding of how herbicides work. Input sellers and farmers generally identify herbicides by the trade name or manufacturer's name and therefore see products with different labels as different herbicides. The active ingredient is displayed on the label in small print and in English only. The products in Figure 18 both contain the same active ingredient, bispyribac-sodium.

Figure 18 Input sellers and farmers need to clearly recognise the active ingredient on herbicide labels.

Repeated use of bispyribac-sodium can lead to a build-up of *Leptochloa chinensis* which is not controlled by this herbicide. A farmer was actually advised by the input seller to switch from B 52 to B 99 to control *L. chinensis* in her rice field. The advice should have been to switch to a different active ingredient such as cyhalofop or fenoxaprop.

It is also important to understand the product formulation (Table 2) as this affects the preparation, mixing and application procedures.

Table 2: Some common herbicide formulations.

EC	Emulsifiable concentrate	SC	Suspension concentrate	SL	Soluble (liquid) concentrate
SP	Soluble powder	WP	Wettable powder	WG	Water dispersible granule

Herbicide efficacy depends on the following:

- application in a timely manner – between planting and crop canopy closure;
- always reading and following the instructions on the product label;
- ensuring the product is suited to the type and stage of crop and weeds to be controlled; and

- ensuring field conditions are suitable.

For example, some products only work when the soil is moist, or when there is standing water or no standing water. The efficacy of post-emergence herbicides is also reduced if the weeds are under water stress.

Herbicide products are designed for early application when weed control is most important to avoid crop losses. Some products are designed to control weeds before they emerge (pre-emergence) while others are only effective after the weeds have emerged (post-emergence).

Farmers should follow herbicide label instructions and:

- use the recommended rate of water;
- use clean fresh water;
- apply the product uniformly across the field;
- ensure nozzles are functioning correctly and providing uniform output;
- minimise drift to non-target areas by using low pressures (<2 bars), by avoiding applications in very strong winds and by limiting water run-off from fields;
- spray perpendicular to the wind so that product is blown away from the applicator;
- rotate herbicide mode of action (MoA) groups to delay the development of herbicide resistance.

Identification of weeds in rice fields

Correct identification of weeds usually requires inspection of features of adult plants, especially reproductive parts. Unfortunately, crop weeds need to be identified when they are very small to enable timely control measures to be taken before planting of crops and to enable choice of appropriate herbicides during early stages of crop growth. Broadleaved weeds can often be identified by the shapes of cotyledonary and first true leaves. Unidentified seedlings can be photographed, tagged and let grow until they can be identified.

Identification of weed seeds in rice seed kept for sowing

The effectiveness of herbicides for weed control can be improved if the weed species likely to be present in the field can be identified before herbicides are applied. This can be achieved by keeping records of weed species present in the previous rice crop in the field. Another option is to inspect harvested paddy or rice seed kept for sowing to identify weed seed contaminants. Images of some important weed seed contaminants of rice as seen in samples of harvested paddy are shown in Figure 19.

Oryza sativa f. spontanea | Fimbristylis miliacea | Echinochloa crus-galli

Echinochloa colona | Cyanotis axillaris | Lindernia antipoda

Melochia corchorifolia | Ischaemum rugosum | Paspalum scrobiculatum

Ludwigia hyssopifolia | Aeschynomene americana | Cyperus iria

Scleria lithosperma | Digitaria bicornis | Actinoscirpus grossus

Figure 19. Some important weed seed contaminants of rice seed as seen in harvested paddy samples (frame size is 8 × 6 mm).

Identification of immature grass weeds in rice fields

Immature grasses are the most difficult weeds to identify in grass crops such as rice. Fortunately, young weedy grass plants can be positively identified by inspecting the collar region of seedlings (Figure 20).

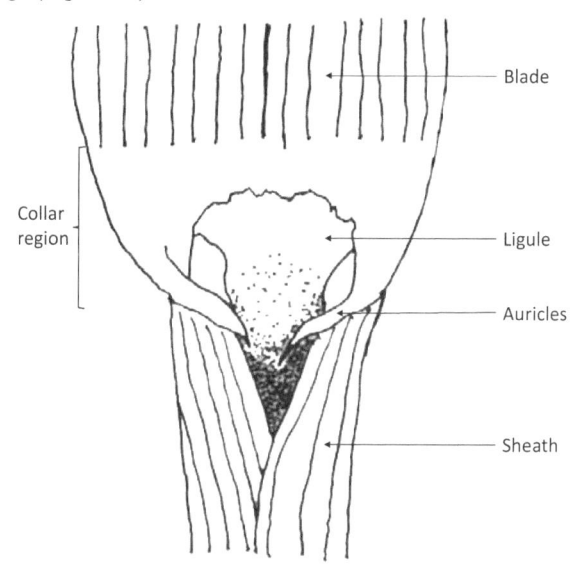

Figure 20. Grass seedlings can be identified by examining the features of the collar region.

For example, rice has a very long membranous ligule as well as prominent auricles (Figure 21). None of the important grass weeds found in Cambodian rice fields have auricles (Figure 21), so any grass seedling without auricles can be assumed to be a weed if found in the rice crop. Importantly, *Echinochloa* spp. have neither auricles nor ligules and can be distinguished from all other grass species in rice fields. Unfortunately, wild and weedy rice also have ligules and auricles and cannot be distinguished from cultivated rice at early growth stages, especially where the crop seed has been broadcast. In drill-planted rice, rice plants growing outside the rows can be assumed to be off-types or weedy rice.

Dactyloctenium aegyptium   *Digitaria bicornis*   *Digitaria ciliaris*   *Echinochloa* spp.

Ischaemum rugosum   *Leptochloa chinensis*   *Oryza sativa*   *Paspalum scrobiculatum*

Figure 21. Collar regions of grass species occurring in rice fields.

Chemical weed control in rice

One hundred per cent of farmers in Battambang province use herbicides (Chhun et al. 2020). Farmers rely heavily on post-emergence herbicides for weed control and few farmers use pre-emergence herbicides. Only 18% of farmers hand weed. Most farmers (72%) who hand weed do so once; only 28% hand weed their field twice.

The most commonly used herbicide is 2,4-D (76%), and 18% of farmers use 2,4-D as the only herbicide. Other herbicides used are bispyribac-sodium (32%), pyribenzoxim (27%), quinclorac + pyrazosulfuron + fenoxaprop (26%), propanil + clomazone (9%) and bensulfuron + quinclorac (2%) (Chhun et al. 2020, Figure 22). Although farmers claim that the grass weed problem is increasing, the predominant herbicide used is 2,4-D, which does not control grasses.

Most farmers (75%) rely on the advice of input sellers for the choice of herbicide (Figure 23). Other sources of information for the surveyed farmers are other farmers (46%), herbicide labels (19%) and chemical companies (8%). Only 30% of farmers are happy with the performance of herbicides, but the remainder did not specify weeds not controlled or why they are not happy.

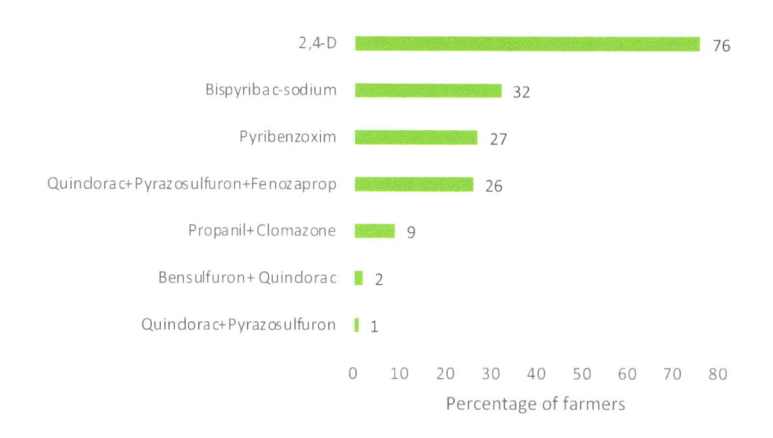

Figure 22. Herbicides used in rice in North West Cambodia.

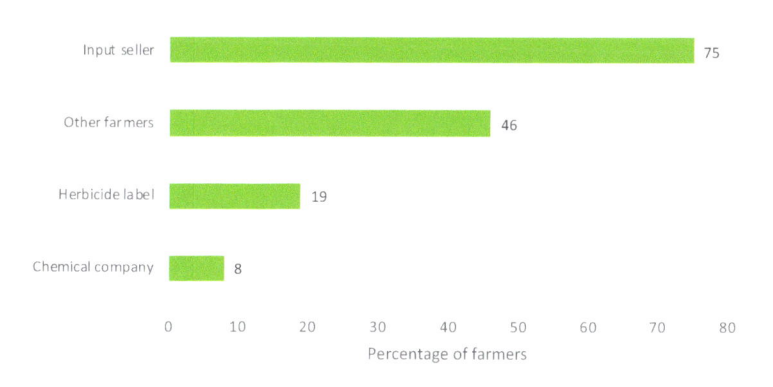

Figure 23. Farmers' source of advice on choice of herbicide.

If the same herbicide active ingredient is applied repeatedly, there is a risk that the species composition of the weed flora in the crop might change to species that are more difficult to control. There is also an increased risk of the development of herbicide resistance. Herbicides can be grouped according to their Mode of Action (MoA) and these are described by the Herbicide Resistance Advisory Committee (HRAC 2023). This knowledge enables rotation between herbicides from different MoA groups to reduce the risk of the development of herbicide resistance (Table 3).

Table 3: Mode of action groups and timing of some herbicides used in DSR in North-West Cambodia.

Herbicide	MoA group (HRAC 2023)	Pre-plant	Post-sowing pre-emergence	Post-emergence
2,4-D	4	✓		✓
Glyphosate	9	✓		
Butachlor	15		✓	
Oxadiazon	14		✓	
Pendimethalin	3		✓	
Pretilachlor	15		✓	
Bispyribac-sodium	2			✓
Bensulfuron + quinclorac	2, 4			✓
Cyhalofop-butyl + florpyrauxifen-benzyl	1, 4			✓
Fenoxaprop + pyrazosulfuron + quinclorac	1, 2, 4			✓
Penoxsulam + florpyrauxifen-benzyl	2, 4			✓
Propanil + clomazone	7, 13			✓
Pyrazosulfuron + quinclorac	2, 4			✓
Pyribenzoxim	2			✓

In North-West Cambodia, thirty-eight per cent of farmers use pre-mixed herbicides, and 68% of farmers use herbicide formulations containing herbicides belonging to MoA Group 2. Weeds readily develop resistance to herbicides in Group 2. For example, resistance to bensulfuron-methyl (Group 2) has been found in *Cyperus difformis* populations in California, and *Echinochloa* spp. have evolved resistance to several herbicides, including bispyribac-sodium (Group 2) (Osuna et al. 2002). The *Echinochloa* case is an example of cross-resistance where the ability of a weed population to express resistance to more than one herbicide. In this case, the *Echinochloa* population had been exposed to Group 2 herbicides but not bispyribac-sodium.

Cyperus iria, *Echinochloa crus-galli*, *E. colona*, *Fimbristylis* spp., *Leptochloa chinensis* and *Oryza sativa* f. *spontanea* are becoming increasing problems. Pre-emergence herbicides enable rotation of herbicide MoA groups as well as providing more timely weed control (Table 4).

Table 4: Mode of action groups, concentration, application timing and application rates for herbicides used in DSR.

Herbicide	MoA group	Active ingredient (%)	Timing (DAS)	Rate (L/ha)
Pre-emergence				
Pretilachlor + fenclorim	15	30+10	0–4	1.0–1.4
Butachlor + fenclorim	15	30 + 10	1–5	0.75–1.0
Pendimethalin	3	33	1–5	3.0
Oxadiazon	14	25	3–5	1.5–2.0
Post-emergence				
Pyribenzoxim	2	5	7–21	0.5–0.6
Propanil + clomazone	7,13	27+12	7–10	1.0
Bispyribac-sodium	2	10	8–15	0.25
Bensulfuron + quinclorac	2,4	5+25	10	1.0
Fenoxaprop + pyrazosulfuron + quinclorac	1,2,4	13+7+50		
Pyrazosulfuron + quinclorac	2,4	3+47		
2,4-D	4	80	21–28	1.0–1.5

Safe use of herbicides

In 2017, 98% of farmers in Battambang province used power backpack sprayers (Chhun et al. 2020). Most farmers use sprayers with a boom fitted with more than one nozzle (average of 5 nozzles per boom). The use of personal protective equipment (PPE) is at a low level of sophistication by Cambodian farmers but includes: facemasks (used by 76% of farmers), hats (73%), long shirts (67%) and gloves (54%). Only 10% of farmers wear boots and none use gas masks or aprons (Chhun et al., 2020, Figure 24).

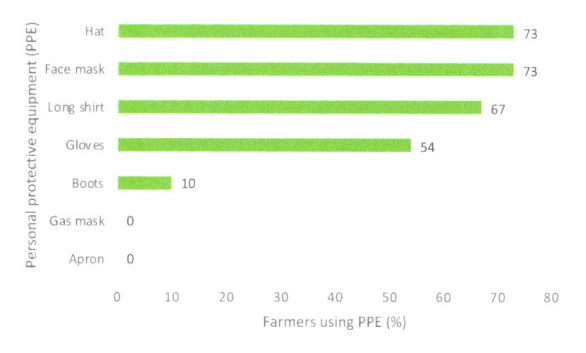

Figure 24. Use of PPE for application of herbicides by farmers in Battambang province.

The spray boom is swept from side in front resulting in the operator becoming saturated with the chemical (Figure 25).

Figure 25. Typical herbicide application technique in Cambodia.

Safe use of herbicides depends on a number of considerations. However, before application safety considerations, it is important that the farmer seeks advice about which herbicide to apply. This is predominantly provided by input sellers or other farmers (Figure 23). Herbicides are registered by the Department of Agricultural Legislation (DAL) and this requires the label to be in Khmer language (Figure 26).

Figure 26. Example of a Cambodian herbicide label.

The label displays: the logo of the manufacturer; important weed species controlled (pictures); the product name; active ingredients (English only); generic safety precautions; instructions for use; registration details; and manufacturer contact details.

It is important to note that the label does not display the active ingredient/s in Khmer or the HRAC herbicide group number. A poster displaying commonly used herbicides according to HRAC MoA groups would be useful.

Guidelines for safe use of herbicides include the following:

1. Read the label;
2. Know the toxicity signal words: Caution- slightly toxic; Warning- moderately toxic; and Danger- highly (not displayed on Khmer labels);
3. Understanding how your herbicide kills and how it is applied will help to prevent mishaps (not displayed on the label);
4. Apply the proper amount. Overuse of herbicides increase toxicity risks and creates unnecessary waste. Conversely, do not under-apply as this will reduce efficacy;
5. Check the weather before application. The best weather for herbicide application is a mild, sunny day with cool temperature and little wind. In Cambodia, these conditions are best met by application in the morning;
6. Wear protective equipment. Protect yourself from chemicals by wearing long pants and shirts, gloves, goggles, and masks while applying herbicide. This will decrease your chance of herbicide exposure. Be sure to wash your clothing, hands, and face well after application;
7. Look for signs of herbicide exposure. Never ingest or have prolonged exposure to herbicides. Symptoms can include skin, eye, or respiratory irritation. Seek medical help if you are concerned or poison control for emergencies;
8. Keep herbicides away from children, pets and livestock to avoid exposure. Read the product label to determine when the treated area can be re-entered. A good rule of thumb is to wait at least until the product dries or 24 hours after application;
9. Do not mix different chemicals unless you know it is safe to do so;
10. Store herbicides in their original packaging with their proper labels and store in a locked container or room. Keep all herbicides out of extreme hot, cold, and damp conditions.

Application of agricultural chemicals using Unmanned Aerial Vehicles (UAVs)

Since around 2019, Unmanned Aerial Vehicle (UAV) spray drones have been rapidly adopted for application of pesticides and nutrient concentrates in rice fields in Cambodia (Figure 27).

Figure 27. Improved pesticide application technique using UAV.

The water volume for herbicide application used by UAV is 20 L/ha compared to 200 L/ha for motorised knapsack sprayers. Application by UAV dramatically reduces the risk of contamination of the operator but increases the risk of off-target damage to crops in adjacent fields as well as having the potential to inflict adverse human and environmental impacts.

The development of the agricultural UAV service provision industry in Cambodia has been primarily driven by the private sector. According to service providers, important benefits of UAV application are: time saving; profitability; operator health; labour saving and ease of application.

A typical UAV service provider has 80 farmer clients, services 350 ha at a rate of 15 minutes per hectare. The median service fee is $10/ha which is competitive with ground application. The most important advantages of UAV over ground application are: application is much quicker than ground application; UAV application avoids problems getting labour for ground application; and the low water volume for UAV does not reduce efficacy.

Important disadvantages of UAV application are: repair and part replacement costs (eg batteries, propellers, motors); and UAV application is affected more by adverse weather. A serious concern for service providers was control failure causing the UAV to crash.

Initially, farmers were reluctant to adopt UAV application and the main reason was that farmers did not believe that UAV application will work as well as ground application. Some farmers are also concerned about the efficacy of low water volumes. Farmers want to see the results first before they decide to adopt UAV application technology.

Service providers agreed that UAV application provided a greater return on investment (ROI) compared to other machinery service provision enterprises. They also agreed that they could recover the UAV purchase cost within 1-2 years.

Predictions of peak adoption of UAV ranged from 15 to 90% with a median of 70%. It appears that the predicted level of adoption had been exceeded by 2023.

Results of weed management research in DSR systems in Cambodia

Weed management and seeding rates

According to the International Rice Research Institute (IRRI), the rice plant population should be in the range of 100–200 plants per square metre (Rickman and Bell n.d.). This means seeding rates might lie between 40 and 100 kg/ha depending on conditions.

Farmers in North-West Cambodia tend to buy new seed sparingly, for example when they change variety or need to restore varietal purity. Otherwise, farmers choose to keep their own seed because of the high seeding rate for hand broadcasting and high cost of clean seed. Seeding rates in DSR can be reduced to as low as 15–25 kg/ha using a precision drill seeder and high-quality seed (Chauhan 2012). If seeding rates can be reduced, farmers might be able to afford to purchase more expensive clean seed from seed producers or seed companies.

Changing from broadcasting to machine drill or row seeding is one way to reduce seeding rates and to enable the purchase of higher quality seed. The lower seeding rate combined with correct placement of seed in the moist seedbed gives drill seeding the additional benefit of reducing the risk of drought-induced crop failure. Wider plant spacing and lower seeding rates are common practices in drought-prone areas (Ahn and Mukelar 1986). At the same time, it is known that wider row spacing and reduced seeding rates reduce rice yields in the presence of weeds (Chauhan and Johnson 2011).

There is a common perception among farmers, as well as some of the scientific community, that increasing rice seeding rates is an effective tool to reduce weed competition in the crop; this is one of the reasons for high seeding rates in North-West Cambodia. However, increasing rice seeding rates of farm-kept seed, contaminated with weed seeds, may actually increase the weed density in the crop and therefore might not reduce weed competition. There is significant potential for re-infestation of fields by sowing rice seeds contaminated with weed seeds, and the ability of the farmer to effectively clean the seed for sowing should also be considered.

Twenty experiments were carried out in Kampong Speu, Kampong Thom, Kampot, Prey Veng and Takeo provinces to determine the effect of varying the seeding method and rate on suppression of weeds (Martin et al. 2020). Ten experiments were carried out in the wet season of 2010 and 10 in the dry season of 2011. The treatments included the traditional farmer practice of hand broadcasting at 180 kg/ha; hand broadcasting at other rates (60, 100, 150, 200, 250 kg/ha); drum seeding at 60 and 80 kg/ha; transplanting two to three 20-day-old seedlings per hill with a spacing of 20 × 20 cm; and transplanting one 10-day-old seedling per hill with a spacing of 25 × 25 cm. In the farmer practice treatment, farmers made their own choice whether or not to weed. Data were collected for weed biomass and paddy yield. Increasing the seeding rate from 60 to 250 kg/ha reduced weed biomass by 46% from 1,742 to 942 kg/ha (Figure 28). However, higher seeding rates expose the crop to losses from drought stress as well as from rice blast disease caused by the fungus *Magnaporthe oryzea* (Onwuchekwa-Henry et al. 2022).

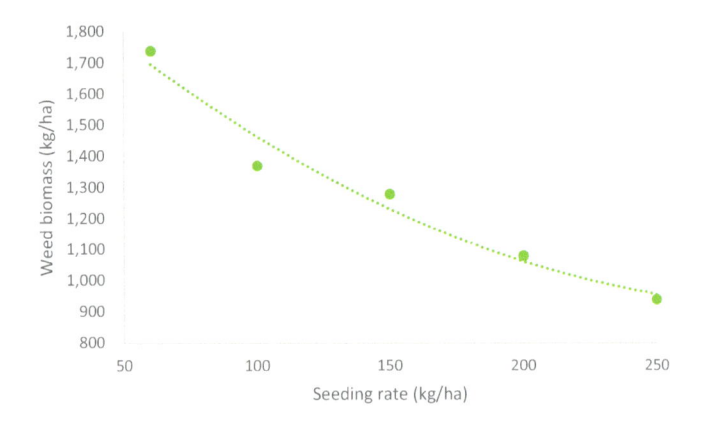

Figure 28. Effect of rice seeding rate on weed biomass.

Weeds reduced average paddy yield from 3,283 to 2,698 kg/ha (22%) and also altered the response to increasing seeding rates. Without weeds, paddy yields increased with seeding rates up to 150 kg/ha, but in the presence of weeds, paddy yields increased with seeding rates up to 200 kg/ha (Figure 29).

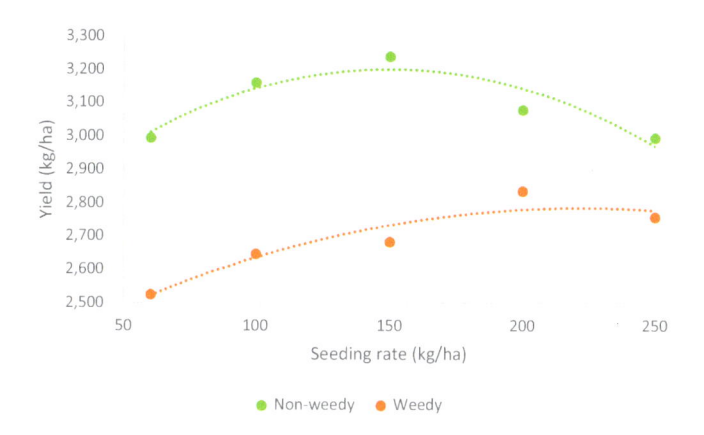

Figure 29. Effect of seeding rate on rice yield with and without weed competition.

The minimum marginal rate of return acceptable to farmers is understood to be between 0.5 and 1.0 (CIMMYT 1988). Drum seeding at 80 kg/ha had the highest marginal rate of return under both weed-free and weedy conditions (Figure 30, Figure 31).

This study suggests that increasing seeding rate alone is not a cost-effective method to reduce paddy yield losses from weed competition and that an integrated approach to weed management should be adopted. For better weed management in wet-seeded rice, row seeding at 80 kg/ha could be combined with reduced inversion tillage, stale seedbed, use of weed-free seed for sowing, and sequential application of pre- and post-emergence herbicides. With an effective integrated weed management strategy, it might be possible to safely reduce seeding rates below 80 kg/ha with seeding machines.

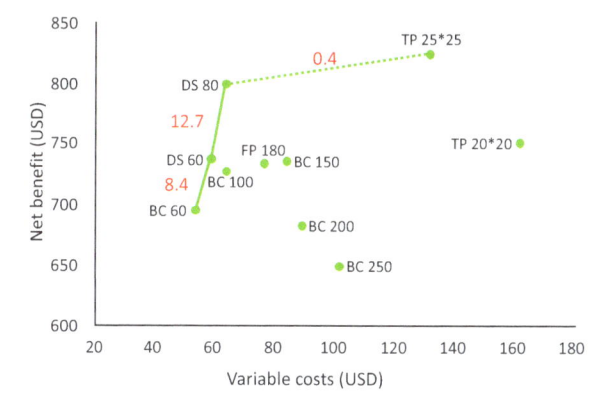

Figure 30. Marginal rates of return (in red) for rice seeding rates (kg/ha) and methods under weed-free conditions.

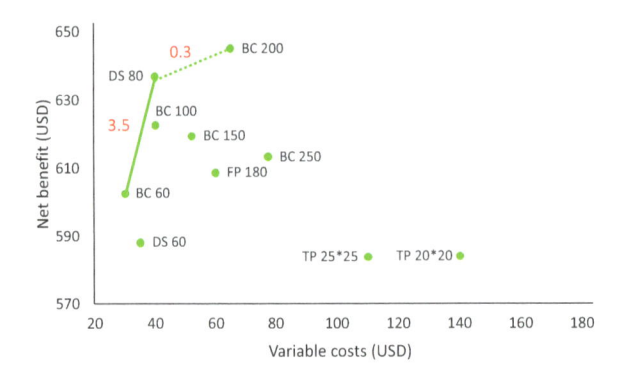

Figure 31. Marginal rates of return (in red) for rice seeding rates (kg/ha) and methods under weedy conditions.

Cambodian rice farmers typically rely on post-emergence herbicides which are often applied later than recommended, especially in crops stressed by the absence of rain or irrigation water after planting. Efficacy of post-emergence herbicides is often sub-optimal on water-stressed weeds. Registered pre-emergence herbicides such as butachlor or pretilachlor applied 0-3 days after sowing control weed seedling emerging with the crop and can reduce the weed pressure on post-emergence herbicides.

Chhun et al. (2020) found that farmer practice for broadcast seeding rates for rice ranged from 100 to 300 kg/ha in Battambang province. Short-duration varieties are broadcast at 300 kg/ha, whereas long-duration varieties such as Neang Khon are broadcast at 100 kg/ha. Sen Kra-ob variety matures in 110 days and is broadcast at 150 kg/ha. With effective weed control, mechanised DSR enables the seeding rate to be reduced accordingly (Table 5).

Table 5. Farmer practice for broadcast seeding of rice and recommended seeding rates for machine planting under weed-free conditions in Battambang province.

Planting method	Duration (days)		
	90	110-120	>120
Broadcast (kg/ha)	300	150	100
Machine (kg/ha)	100	75	50

Weed management in wet DSR

Five weed management treatments were included in the experimental design of Then et al. 2023. The five treatments included an integrated pest management (IPM) option comprising wet tillage, good land leveling after ploughing, use of good quality seed, sowing by drum seeder with 20 cm distance between rows and fertiliser management according to recommendations based on soil type (Blair and Blair 2014). A low seeding rate compared to farmer practice was used but with adaptations to the local preferences, 100, 120, and 110 kg/ha in Battambang, Kampong Thom and Prey Veng provinces, respectively.

The herbicide regime for improved practice was pretilachlor + fenclorim (0.3 kg a.i./ha) applied at 1 L/ha at 0-3 DAS, followed by fenoxaprop + ethoxysulfuron (0.088 kg a.i./ha) at 870 mL/ha. The conventional practice treatment was based on the average of 40 surveyed farmers randomly selected from the village (Flor et al. 2020). Based on the survey, conventional practice was application of the herbicide quinclorac 47% + pyrazosulfuron-ethyl 3%, applied at 10, 20 and 30 DAS in Battambang, at 7 and 14 DAS in Kampong Thom and at 7 and 15 DAS in Prey Veng. The farmer-practice seeding rates were broadcast at 180, 240, and 335 kg/ha in Battambang, Kampong Thom and Prey Veng provinces respectively.

Timely weed control with pre-emergence herbicides can allow the reduction of rice seeding rates. Farmer practice broadcast seeding rates at the experimental sites ranged from 180 to 335 kg/ha whereas improved practice, employing the use of a drum seeder, reduced the range of seeding rates to 100 to 120 kg/ha and this represented a cost saving for seed of 19 to 51 USD/ha.

The improved management systems reduced weed biomass from 22 to 11 kg/ha (Figure 32) and produced an average paddy yield of 4,830 kg/ha compared with 3,810 kg/ha for farmer practice, an increase of 1,020 kg/ha (Figure 33).

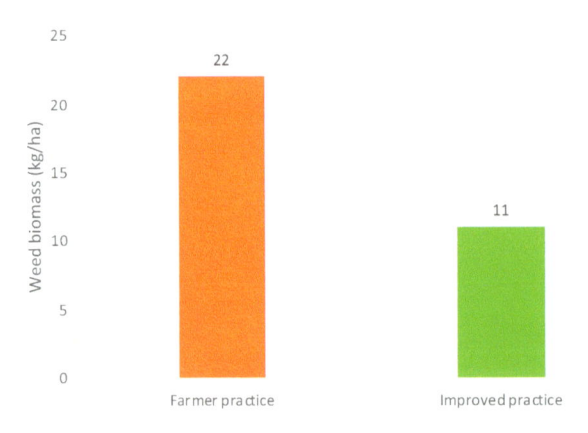

Figure 32. Comparison of improved practice vs farmer practice for reduction of weed biomass.

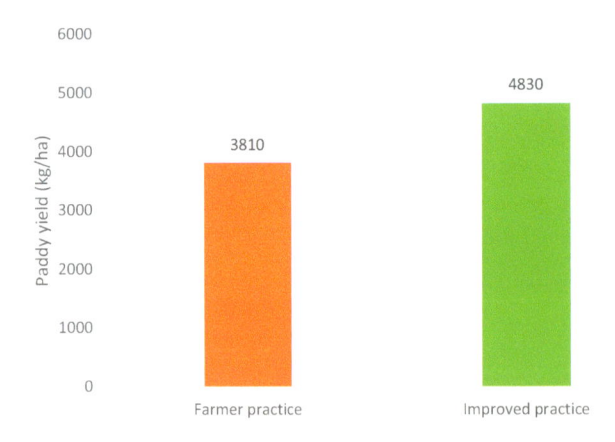

Figure 33. Comparison of improved practice vs farmer practice weed management
for effect on rice paddy yield.

The input costs for improved practice were 56 USD/ha less than for farmer practice, income got improved practice was 25% greater than for farmer practice resulting in a net return for improved practice 75% greater than for farmer practice (Figure 34).

Figure 34. Effect of improved weed management practice on input costs, total revenue and net benefit for rice.

These results are consistent with the work of Martin et al. (2020) with wet DSR in Cambodia showing that seeding rates can be reduced from 200 to 80 kg/ha or less with row or drill seeding under effective weed management.

Weed management in dry DSR

Although registered and available, pre-emergence herbicides suitable for dry DSR such as butachlor, oxadiazon and pendimethalin are not commonly used for weed control in rice in North-West Cambodia. Experiments to evaluate herbicides applied post-sowing pre-emergence for weed control in dry direct-seeded rice were carried out during the wet seasons of 2018 and 2019 in Battambang province. The pre-emergence herbicides tested were butachlor, oxadiazon and pendimethalin. The post-emergence herbicide used was bispyribac-sodium. Herbicides were applied in a water volume of 350 L/ha using an electric-powered knapsack sprayer.

Weed density at 34 DAS was not effectively reduced by post-emergence herbicide alone but all pre-emergence herbicides gave satisfactory weed control when followed by post-emergence herbicide. Oxadiazon alone did not significantly reduce weed numbers (Figure 35). Application of butachlor + bispyribac-sodium gave a paddy yield of 5,037 kg/ha compared to bispyribac-sodium alone (4,049 kg/ha). Post-emergence herbicide alone gave a yield increase from 3,673 to 4,049 kg/ha (Figure 36).

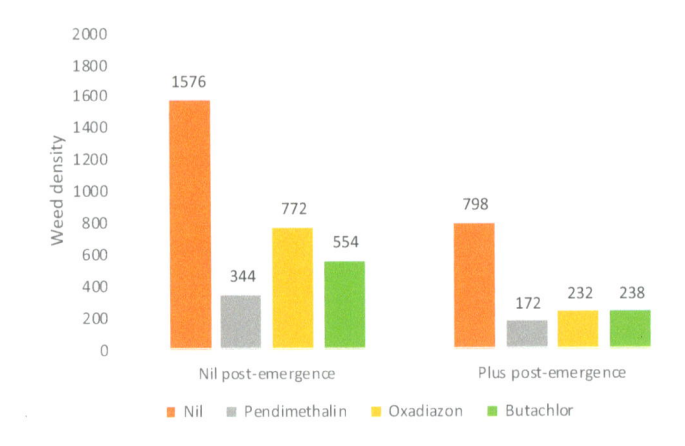

Figure 35. Effect of pre-and post-emergence emergence herbicides on weed density at 34 DAS (plants/m^2).

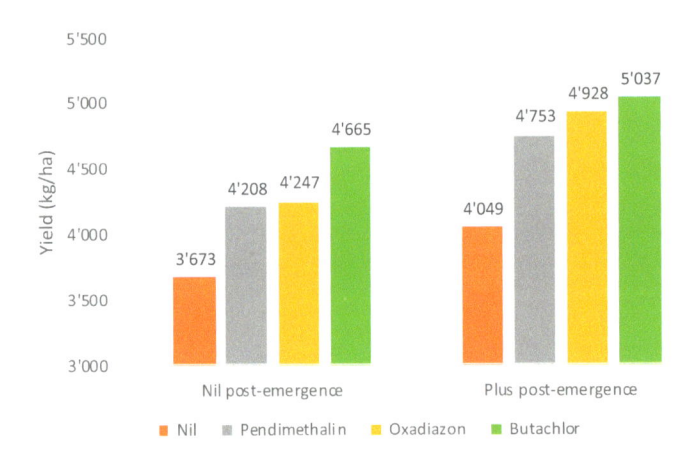

Figure 36. Effect of pre- and post-emergence herbicides on rice paddy yield (kg/ha).

Research and development priorities for weed management in rice in Cambodia

Background

Weed research issues, challenges, and opportunities in Cambodia should be considered in the light of current and expected changes in agricultural production systems as affected by social, economic, physical and environmental interactions. Strategies for weed management in Cambodia's agricultural systems should take account of the effect of rapid socio-economic changes on production systems and the livelihoods of smallholder farmers. Optimal weed management strategies and research priorities need to be developed in line with rapidly changing agricultural systems associated with:

- Climate variability and climate change;
- Land clearance and development of new agricultural systems;
- The need for sustainable intensification and diversification in existing agricultural systems;
- Migration of labour from rural areas and the drive towards modernization of agriculture;
- Economics of production and efficiency of scale.

Weeds should be managed using an integrated weed management (IWM) approach that combines all available options throughout the crop cycle. The aims should be to keep weed numbers low and prevent weeds from producing seeds throughout the cropping cycle: The elements of IWM in DSR rice systems include:

- Removal of weed seeds and vegetative material from machines before moving them from field to field;
- Planting crop seed free of weed seeds and checking of any purchased seed for weed seed contamination;
- Planting in rows to enable inter-row control of weeds;
- Application of pre-emergence herbicides and timely application of post-emergence herbicides according to label directions;
- Hand-weeding during crop growth, especially at anthesis to prevent weeds setting seed with special attention being given to weedy rice (*Oryza sativa* f. *spontanea*);
- Control of weeds on bunds, channels and other areas surrounding rice fields with special attention being given to removing wild rice (eg *O. rufipogon*);
- Employment of the principles of Conservation Agriculture (CA): reduced soil disturbance, crop rotations and retention of crop residues at the soil surface;
- Avoiding inversion tillage which results in the burial and induced dormancy of weed seeds;
- Employment of the stale seedbed technique and, where possible, planting cover crops during the early dry season;
- Replacing pre-sowing tillage, where possible, with herbicide application to avoid weed seeds germinating at the same time as the crop.

In Cambodia, development of future research priorities must take account of the lack of uptake of existing published research by Government agencies and their failure to incorporate results of new research into extension media. In addition, multiple conflicting messages emanating from Donors and NGOs confuse farmers and delay adoption of good agricultural practices (GAP). Furthermore, in the absence of a functioning public extension service, Cambodian farmers are locked into pesticide-reliant practices and limited use of alternatives. Pesticide manufacturers, distributors and local sellers reinforce pesticide-based recommendations as the dominant technology (Flor et al. 2020).

Although care should be taken to not duplicate previous research, action should be taken to ensure that important results of published research are reported to policy makers and demonstrated to farmers. Therefore, priorities can be placed under the separate headings of "demonstration" and "research". Care should be taken to avoid basic or "academic" research where results cannot be applied directly to rice production under Cambodian conditions.

Demonstration

- Use of pre-emergence herbicides and timely application of post-emergence herbicides in direct-seeded rice;
- Importance of effective weed control to enable reduced seeding rates in mechanized direct-seeding of rice;
- Options to reduce weed seed and weedy rice contamination in rice seed kept for sowing.

Research

- Development of management practices to reduce weed seed banks in direct-seeded rice fields;
- Integrated weed management strategies to delay or avoid development of herbicide resistance in major weed species in direct-seeded rice;
- Options for the integrated management of weedy rice (*Oryza sativa* f. *spontanea*) in direct-seeded rice;
- Comparison of UAV (20 L/ha) with ground application (200 L/ha) for efficacy of pre- and post-emergence herbicides in rice.

Acknowledgements

This publication draws upon recent research on weed management in direct-seeded rice in Cambodia. This includes the findings of projects CSE/2009/039 and CSE/2015/044 funded by the Australian Centre for International Agricultural Research (ACIAR). Information was also sourced from research completed by the Ecologically based Participatory Integrated Pest Management for Rice in Cambodia (EPIC) implemented by the International Rice Research Institute (IRRI) and funded by the United States Agency for International Development (USAID) (AIDOOA-L-15-00001), under the Feed the Future IPM Innovation Laboratory. IRRI has also provided support for planting machine comparisons under the CGIAR Initiative: Excellence in Agronomy (EiA).

References

Ahn S.W. and Mukelar A. 1986. Rice blast management under upland conditions, in *Progress in upland rice research: proceedings of the 1985 Jakarta Conference*, International Rice Research Institute, Manila, Philippines.

Beecher G., Johnson D., Desbiolles J., North S., Singh R., Som B., Ngin C., Janiya J., Dunn T., Seng V., et al. 2014. A policy dialogue on rice futures: Rice-based farming systems research in the Mekong region. Proceedings of a dialogue held in Phnom Penh, Cambodia, 7–9 May 2014. In ACIAR Proceedings Series; Australian Centre for International Agricultural Research: Canberra, Australia, 2014; p. 158.

Chauhan B.S. 2012. *Weed management in direct-seeded rice systems*, International Rice Research Institute, Los Baños, Philippines.

Chauhan B.S., Ahmed S., Awan T.H., Jabran K., and Manalil S. 2015. Integrated weed management approach to improve weed control efficiencies for sustainable rice production in dry-seeded systems. *Crop Protection* **71**, 19-24.

Chauhan B.S. and Johnson D.E. 2011. Row spacing and weed control timing affect yield of aerobic rice. *Field Crops Research* **121**, 226–231.

Chhim C., Buth B. and Ear S. 2015. Effect of labour movement on agricultural mechanisation in Cambodia, Cambodia Development Resource Institute Working Paper Series No. 107, CDRI, Phnom Penh.

Chhun S., Kumar V., Martin R.J., Srean P. and Hadi B.A.R. 2020. Weed management practices of smallholder rice systems in Northwest Cambodia. *Crop Protection* **135**:104793, Doi: 10.1016/j.cropro.2019.04.017.

Davidson P.J.A. 2006. The Biodiversity of the Tonle Sap Biosphere Reserve 2005 status review. Technical output of the UNDP/GEF-funded Tonle Sap Conservation Project.

2006. Available online: http://s3.amazonaws.com/WCSResources/file_20120710_00450.

Flor R.J., Maat H., Hadi B.A.T., Then R., Kraus E., et al. 2020. How do stakeholder interactions in Cambodian rice farming villages contribute to a pesticide lock-in? *Crop Protection* **135**, 104799, https://doi.org/10.1016/j.cropro.2019.04.023.

Heap I. 2014. Global perspective of herbicide-resistant weeds. Pest Management Science 70, Special Issue: Global Herbicide Resistance Challenge: pp 1306-1315. https://doi.org/10.1002/ps.3696.

HRAC. 2023. Global herbicide classification lookup. https://hracglobal.com/tools/classification-lookup/?s=cyhalofop&mode=&letter=&number=#classificationLookup.

Ikeda H., Kamoshita A., Yamagishi J., Ouk M., Lor B. 2008. Assessment of management of direct seeded rice production under different water conditions in Cambodia. Paddy Water Environ 6, 91–103. DOI 10.1007/s10333-007-0103-9.

Jabran K. and Chauhan B.S. 2015. Weed management in aerobic rice systems. Crop Prot 78:151–163.

Kachroo D. and Bazaya B.R. 2011. Efficacy of different herbicides on growth and yield of direct wet seeded rice sown through drum seeder. *Indian J. Weed Sci* **43**, 67-69.

Khaliq A. and Matloob A. 2012. Weed crop competition period in three fine rice cultivars under direct seeded rice culture. *Pakistan Journal of Weed Science Research* **17**, 229-243.

Khun L.H. and Soly S. 2012. National Seed Standards. General Directorate of Agriculture, Ministry of Agriculture Forestry and Fisheries, Royal Government of Cambodia, Phnom Penh, Cambodia.

Martin R.J. 2020. Weed research issues, challenges, and opportunities in Cambodia. *Crop Protection* **124**. DOI: 10.1016/j.cropro.2017.06.019

Martin R., Chhun S., Yous S., Rien R., Korn C., Srean, P. 2021. Survey of Weed Management Practices in Direct-Seeded Rice in North-West Cambodia. *Agronomy* **11**, 498. https://doi.org/10.3390/agronomy11030498.

Martin R.J., Som B., Janiya J., Rien R., Yous S., Chhun S. and Korn C. 2020. Integrated Management of weeds in direct-seededrRice in Cambodia. *Agronomy* **10**, 1557; doi:10.3390/agronomy10101557.

Martin R.J., Van Ogtrop F., Henson Y., Broeum K.R., Rien, R., Srean, P. and, Tan D.K.Y. 2017. A survey of weed seed contamination of rice paddy in Cambodia. *Weed Research* **57**, 333–341, doi:10.1111/wre.12265.

Matsukawa M., Ito K., Kawakita K. et al 2016. Current status of pesticide use among rice farmers in Cambodia. *Appl Entomol Zool* **51**, 571–579 (2016). https://doi.org/10.1007/s13355-016-0432-5.

Nesbitt H.J. and Chan P. 1997. Rice-based farming systems. In: Rice Production in Cambodia (ed. HJ NESBITT), 31–38. International Rice Research Institute, Manila, Philippines.

Onwuchekwa-Henry C., Van Ogtrop F.F., Tan D.K.Y. 2022. Seeding rate, fertiliser and herbicide effects on canopy growth and productivity of direct-seeded rice (DSR) under different management practices. Field Crops Research 284. DOI: 10.1016/j.fcr.2022.108565.

Osuna M.D., Vidotto F., Fischer A.J., Bayer D.E., De Prado R. and Ferrero A. 2002. Cross-resistance to bispyribac-sodium and bensulfuron-methyl in *Echinochloa phyllopogon* and *Cyperus difformis*, *Pesticide Biochemistry and Physiology* **73**, 9–17.

Rawat A., Chaudhary C.S., Upadhyaya V.B. and Jain V. 2012. Efficacy of bispyribac-sodium on weed flora and yield of drilled rice. *Indian Journal of Weed Science* **44**, 183–185.

Rickman J. and Bell M. n.d. *Seed rate (high)*, Rice Knowledge Bank website, accessed 24 July 2022. http://knowledgebank.irri.org/decision-tools/rice-doctor/rice-doctor-fact-sheets/item/seed-high-rate.

Singh M., Bhullar M.S. and Chauhan B.S. 2014. The critical period for weed control in dry-seeded rice. *Crop Protection* **66**, 80-85, ISSN 0261-2194, available at https://doi.org/10.1016/j.cropro.2014.08.009.

Singh V., Jat M.L., Ganie Z.A., Chauhan BS and Gupta RK 2016. Herbicide options for effective weed management in dry direct-seeded rice under scented rice-wheat rotation of western Indo-Gangetic Plains. *Crop Protection* **81**, 168-176, 10.1016/j.cropro.2015.12.021.

Then R., Flor R.J., Hady B., Kumar V., Chou C., Chhay K., Choun S., Chhun S., Voeun S., Vath K., Long K., Martin R.J. 2023. Efficacy of alternative weed management recommendations for direct wet-seeded rice systems in Cambodia. In preparation.

Wongtamee A., Maneechote C., Pusadee T., Rerkasem B., Jamjod S. 2017. The dynamics of spatial and temporal population genetic structure of weedy rice (*Oryza sativa* f. *spontanea* Baker). *Genetic Resources and Crop Evolution* 64, 23-39.

Publisher: Eliva Press Global Ltd

Email: info@elivapress.com

Eliva Press is an independent international publishing house established for the publication and dissemination of academic works worldwide. The company provides high quality and professional service to all our authors.

Our Services:
Free of charge, open-minded, eco-friendly, innovational.

-Free standard publishing services (manuscript review, step-by-step book preparation, publication, distribution, and marketing).
-No financial risk. The author does not have to pay any hidden fees for publication.
-Editors. Dedicated editors will assist step by step through the projects.
-Money paid to the author for every book sold. Up to 50% royalties guaranteed.
-ISBN (International Standard Book Number). We assign a unique ISBN to every Eliva Press book.
-Digital archive storage. Books will be available online for a long time. We don't need to have a stock of our titles. No unsold copies. Eliva Press uses environment friendly print on demand technology that limits the needs of publishing business. We care about environment and share these principles with our customers.
-Cover design. Cover art is designed by a professional designer.
-Worldwide distribution. We continue expanding our distribution channels to make sure that all readers have access to our books.
-Marketing tools. We provide marketing tools such as banners, paid advertising, social media promotion and more.

Printed in the USA
CPSIA information can be obtained
at www.ICGtesting.com
LVHW062006110124
768768LV00001B/12

9 7 8 9 9 9 4 9 8 7 9 9 3